Nathaniel
Maclise

The Berenstain Bears®
and the
BABY CHIPMUNK

Stan & Jan Berenstain

Reader's Digest **Kids**

Westport, Connecticut

One day the Bear family was outside enjoying the sunshine.

Papa was resting.

Mama was working in the garden.

Brother and Sister were
playing catch.

"Look!" said Sister. "A
mouse!"

"That's not a mouse,"
said Brother.

"If it's not a mouse, what is it?" asked Sister.

"It's a chipmunk," said Mama. "A *baby* chipmunk."

"May we keep him, Mama?" cried Sister. "May we? May we? Please!"

"Look," said Brother. "His eyes aren't even open yet!"

"That's right," said Mama. "This baby should be with his mother. But she won't come for him if she sees us here. Let's hide behind our tree house for a while and see if she comes."

The Bears
watched and
watched. But the
mother chipmunk
did not come.

"Now may we keep him?" cried
Sister. "May we? May we? Please?"

"I think we shall have to," said
Mama. "At least for a while."

"That's right," said Papa. "Babies
need to be fed and kept warm."

"Papa, do you have a clean
hanky?" asked Mama.

Mama picked up the baby
chipmunk and tucked him into
Papa's hanky.

Then she carried the baby
chipmunk into the house. Papa,
Sister, and Brother followed.

"Sister," said Mama,
"please get one of your doll's
baby bottles. And Brother,
get some milk and honey."

The baby chipmunk was very hungry. As he drank from the bottle, he opened his eyes. They were big and brown.

"Let's name him Brown Eyes," said Sister.

"That's as good a name as any," said Mama.

Sister took a turn feeding Brown Eyes.

Papa got a box for a bed,
and Brother made it cozy.

Brown Eyes liked his new bed.
Soon he was fast asleep.

The next morning Sister and Brother ran downstairs to see their new pet. His bed was there. But he was not. They looked all around.

"There he is!" said Brother.
Brown Eyes was up on the table.
He had knocked over the sugar bowl
and was eating the sugar.
"I guess he needs more than milk
and honey," said Sister.

The cubs went outside and
gathered some seeds.

Brown Eyes was very
small, but he had big
chipmunk teeth. Just like
that, those seeds were gone!

Brown Eyes loved to play.
But what he loved most
was exploring.

He explored Mama's vegetable bin.

He explored Papa's desk.

He explored Mama's sewing basket.

Then one day he explored one place too many. He explored Papa's pant leg—all the way up to the knee.

And while he was up there, he
tried out his big sharp teeth.

"You know what I think," said Mama. "I think Brown Eyes is telling us he's not a baby anymore. He's telling us he's big enough to go out in the world and join his friends."

"But, Mama!" said Sister. "I don't want him to go. I love him so!"

"We all love him," said Mama.
"But it really isn't fair to make him
a pet. Chipmunks need
to be free. They
need to explore.

"Inside," said Mama, "there are not many good places to explore."

The cubs thought about— Mama's vegetable bin,

Papa's desk,

Mama's
sewing basket,

and Papa's pant leg.

"Outside," said Mama, "Brown Eyes
will be able to explore all of nature."
As usual, Mama was right.

The cubs didn't even have to say good-bye. They saw Brown Eyes almost every day, playing with his friends and exploring nature—right in their own backyard.